Algy's Amazing
Adventures
IN THE
ARCTIC

Look out for

Algy's Amazing Adventures
IN THE

Algy's Amazing Adventures

IN THE

ARCTIC

Kaye Umansky

Illustrated by
Richard Watson

Orion
Children's Books

First published in Great Britain in 2013
by Orion Children's Books
a division of the Orion Publishing Group Ltd
Orion House
5 Upper Saint Martin's Lane
London WC2H 9EA
An Hachette UK Company

1 3 5 7 9 10 8 6 4 2

Text © Kaye Umansky 2013
Illustrations © Richard Watson 2013

The right of Kaye Umansky and Richard Watson to be
identified
as author and illustrator of this work has been asserted.

The Orion Publishing Group's policy is to use papers that
are natural, renewable and recyclable products and made
from wood grown in sustainable forests. The logging and
manufacturing processes are expected to conform to the
environmental regulations of the country of origin.

A catalogue record for this book is available
from the British Library.

Printed and bound in China

www.orionbooks.co.uk

To Freya and Elinor

Contents

Chapter One

This is Algy, short for Algernon Pugh. He is named after his granddad and wishes he wasn't.

This is Cherry Smellie. She lives next door. She is Algy's best friend, and she loves adventures.

Which is just as well, because Algy has discovered something amazing!

At the bottom of his garden
is a shed. In that shed is a loose
plank. And behind that plank is…

Another world!

Algy wasn't in a good mood. At breakfast, Mum had told him that Aunty Sue was coming to visit – with Dawn.

Dawn was Algy's cousin.

Algy didn't like small children. They had runny noses. They were bad at sharing. They had temper tantrums and broke people's toys. Well, Dawn did.

He hurried into the garden to meet Cherry. Maybe an adventure would cheer him up.

Cherry was waiting outside the shed. A small boy wearing a little red baseball cap was with her. His nose was running and he was holding a carrot.

Hmm, thought Algy.

"Who's this?" he said.

"My brother, Bradley," said Cherry.

Algy was annoyed. He had been looking forward to another adventure. He didn't want a little kid trailing along.

"Say hello to Algy, Brad," said Cherry.

Brad said nothing.

"What did you bring him for?" said Algy.

"His playgroup's closed and Mum's busy," said Cherry.

"Well, he can't come with us. He's too little. He'll get in the way," said Algy.

"He'll be okay," said Cherry.
"You'll be good, won't you, Brad?"
Brad still said nothing.

Algy didn't think he would be
good at all. He'd cry and make a
fuss, just like Dawn always did.

"I don't think it's a good idea,"
said Algy.

"Well, at least we can look," said Cherry. "See what's there today."

Algy stared down at Brad. Brad Smellie. It wasn't a great name.

Brad looked up and gave a sudden smile.

Algy didn't smile back. He just snapped, "Come on, then," and walked into the shed.

Brad followed behind.

The three of them stood before
the loose plank.

"Go on," said Cherry.

Algy's heart was beating fast.
What would be there this time?

He reached out and pushed.
The plank fell outwards. And
through the gap, they saw…

"Snow!" gasped Cherry. "It's snowing!"

Hmm, thought Algy.

Chapter Two

Soft white flakes were falling in a wintry landscape of fir trees. The ground was a thick carpet without a single footprint.

Before Cherry or Algy could
stop him, Brad squeezed through
the gap and out into the snow.

"Come back!" shouted Algy.
"It might be dangerous!"

Typical, he thought. Little kids
just do what they like.

"Oh, let him," said Cherry.
"He loves snow."
Brad was laughing and
bouncing around, kicking up snow.
"Wheee!" he shouted. "Wheeee!"

"Stay there, we're coming!"
shouted Cherry. "Come on, Algy,
let's make a snowman!"

Algy thought about this. It didn't *look* like there was anything to worry about. But what if there were wolves? Or bears? He had once seen a television programme about huge hairy man-beasts who roamed the Arctic. Yetis, they were called. Although nobody had ever seen one.

Still. Building a snowman sounded like fun. They wouldn't go far. They could stay right by the shed, in case of emergencies.

A rusty spade was propped against the shed wall. He grabbed it and squeezed through the gap.

Chapter Three

Building the snowman kept Algy
warm. He was enjoying himself.
Cherry patted the snow in place.
Brad ran around, singing loudly.

"If ya happy an' ya know it, clappya hans," sang Brad.

He was being really good, compared to Dawn, Algy thought. So far, anyway.

"Now we need a hat," said Cherry. She took off Brad's cap and placed it on the snowman's head.

Brad giggled.

Algy reached into his pocket. There were two conkers in there. He pressed them into the snowman's face.

"Eyes! Funny!" shouted Brad. He really was much easier to please than Dawn.

"Where's your carrot, Brad?" asked Cherry. "We need it."

Algy found the carrot lying in the snow.

"Here," he said, passing it to Brad. "His nose. You put it on."

Brad carefully set the carrot
in place. The three of them stood
back to admire their work.

"Good," said Brad proudly.

"Now what?" said Cherry.
"Shall we go exploring?"

Algy stared into the silent pine trees. For some reason, they made him nervous.

"I don't think we should," said Algy.

"Oh, come on," said Cherry.

"I'm freezing," said Algy. "My feet are like blocks of ice."

"Let's pop back and get coats," said Cherry. "Mum will kill me if Brad catches a cold."

"All right," said Algy. "But we stay in sight of the shed."

"Fine. Brad, we're going home."

"No," said Brad.

Uh oh, thought Algy. Here we go. Tantrum coming up.

"We'll come straight back," said Cherry. "You want to be warm, don't you, if we're going exploring?"

"No," said Brad. He wrapped his arms around the snowman.

"Well, you can't stay here," said Cherry. "Can he, Algy?"

Algy looked at Brad. It was a good snowman and Brad didn't want to be parted from him. Understandable, really.

"I suppose he could wait in the shed," said Algy.

Brad looked uncertain.

"I've got sweets at home," said Algy. "I'll bring you some."

"Okay," said Brad. He crunched over and took Algy's hand.

"Wow!" said Cherry. "He likes you."

"Likes sweets, you mean," said Algy. But he felt pleased.

Chapter Four

Five minutes later, Cherry and
Brad were back at the shed,
wearing their winter coats.

"I've brought Brad's jacket,"
Cherry said. "And mittens."

"I've got the sweets," said Algy.
They hurried inside.

The shed was empty. Cold air blew through the gap.

There was no sign of Brad.

"Where is he?" asked Algy crossly. "We told him to stay here."

Why couldn't little kids ever do what they were told? Well, Brad wasn't getting any sweets now, that was for sure.

"Hiding, probably," said Cherry. "He does that."

They squeezed through the gap into the cold, white, silent world beyond.

It had stopped snowing. All was still, apart from the odd soft plop as snow slipped off branches.

The snowman was there, staring at them with his conker eyes. But…

"The carrot's gone," said Cherry. "And Brad's cap." She shouted, "Brad? Where are you? "

Silence. And then…

"oOOOOOwwwwoooo!"

"What was that?" gasped Cherry.

Algy said nothing. The hairs were standing up on the back of his neck. And not just because of that awful cry.

"Brad?" shouted Cherry again.

"Cherry," said Algy.

"What?"

"Look."

There, leading away from the snowman, were huge footprints! They definitely weren't Brad's, and they disappeared into the trees.

"Oh!" Cherry sounded shocked. "What do you think made those?"

"I don't know," said Algy. "But whatever it is, it's taken Brad."

A short way ahead of them, half-buried in the snow, was a little red cap.

Chapter Five

Cherry picked up the cap without a word. She looked upset. It wasn't every day you lost a little brother, Algy supposed.

Cherry was his friend and he had to help her. He grabbed the spade, which was lying next to the snowman. It wasn't a great weapon, but it was better than nothing.

"Right," Algy said. "Let's go and find him."

They trudged towards the trees, following the giant footprints. When Algy looked back he saw that the shed was already out of sight.

It was dark in the pine forest. Algy wished he hadn't seen that television programme now. The one about Yetis. The ones that didn't exist.

Suddenly, Cherry stopped. The footprints led across a frozen lake. Trees grew thickly around the edge. There was no way around.

"Now what?" asked Cherry.

"We cross," said Algy. "If it's thick enough to take the weight of whatever made those footprints, it should be safe."

He didn't like the thought of meeting whatever had taken Brad. But he also didn't like thinking about what Cherry's mum would say if they went home without him.

They stepped out onto the slippery ice. Algy tried using the spade for balance, but it broke, so he threw it away.

They had nearly made it across the lake when the distant howl came again.

"oOOOOOWwwwoooo!"
Cherry grabbed Algy in fright,
and he fell over.

"Keep calm," he said,
struggling to get back up. "We're
nearly there."

Slipping and sliding, they finally reached the other side.

The huge footprints stood out in the snow. They led away up a hill.

Algy's legs ached as they puffed up the slope.

At the top, a nasty surprise was waiting for them.

They were standing on the edge of a deep cliff – and strung across it was a rope bridge!

Chapter Six

The side ropes of the bridge looked frayed, and the wooden slats were slippery with snow. In a few places, they were missing altogether.

Cherry stepped forward. Algy
grabbed her arm.

"Wait! It's snowing again. Your
glasses will get all snowed up. Just
hold the ropes and follow me."

Algy could hardly believe he had said that. He hated heights. He seemed to become a different person when he was on an adventure.

The bridge wobbled as he stepped onto it.

Slowly, carefully, they began to cross. The ropes creaked and the snow blew in their faces.

They had almost reached the middle when Algy stopped.

"What?" said Cherry. "What?"

"Listen," said Algy. "Can't you hear it?"

"If ya happy an' ya know it, clappya hans…"

"It's him!" shouted Cherry. "It's Brad! Hurry!"

"All right, take it easy," said Algy. Brad sounded okay, but what had happened to the owner of those giant footprints? "Stay where you are, Brad! We're coming!"

"Brad, where are you?" said Cherry, as they reached the far side.

"There," said Algy, pointing.

Brad was sitting on a tree stump, swinging his legs and waving.

"Brad!" Cherry ran and threw her arms around him. "What happened? Are you all right?"

"Ess," said Brad. "De furry man eated my cawwot. Gone now." He pointed to the giant footsteps, which led away into distant trees.

Algy and Cherry looked at each other.

"What furry man?" asked Algy.

"Funny furry man," said Brad. "Gived me a wide. Where de sweeties?"

"Here," said Algy. He took the sweets out of his pocket and handed them to Brad. "All for you."

Brad shook his head.

"No," he said. "For hungry furry man. Nicer dan cawwot." He placed the sweets in a pile on the stump. "Are we goin' home now?"

"We are," said Cherry. "Hold out your arms, I'll put your coat on."

Right then, the sun came out from behind the clouds and the world sparkled.

"Come on, Brad," said Algy. "I'll give you a piggy back."

Chapter Seven

That night, Algy lay in bed
thinking about the adventure.

Getting home had been easy.
Going over the rope bridge again
had been no problem, even with
Brad on his back.

The frozen pond had been fun. Cherry had slipped over this time, bringing them all down with her. They'd laughed and laughed.

In the end Aunty Sue hadn't made it after all. Algy wasn't sorry. He was glad to give Dawn a miss.

Not all little kids were a pain, though. Brad was okay. Fun to have around, actually.

He wouldn't mind him coming on another adventure.

Algy looked again at the
picture Brad had drawn for him.
Hmm.

What are you going to read next?

More adventures with

or go to sea with

Horrid Henry,

Poppy the Pirate Dog,

or into space with

You could have fun on

Cudweed.

A Rainbow Shopping Day,

or explore

Down in the Jungle,